BRATZ™

Party Perfection!

The Bratz Party Handbook

Executive Brand Editor,
Charles O'Connor

Used under licence by Penguin Young Readers Group
Published in Great Britain by Ladybird Books Ltd 2004
80 Strand, London WC2R 0RL
A Penguin Company
10 9 8 7 6 5 4 3 2 1
Printed in the USA
LADYBIRD and the device of a Ladybird are the
trademarks of Ladybird Books Ltd.

Party Schedule

It's Party*Time!

We don't just go to parties!

We are the party!

You don't need a lot of money to throw a party with total cutting-edge appeal. All you need are good friends, good eats, and a few quick and clever ideas for making your party one your pals will never forget! Lucky for you, the secrets to party perfection are all right here!

so stop talking already!

yeah! Let's get the party started!

We're as good as **there**!
Turn the page
and let the fun begin...

In with the New!

It's the New Year, and you know what they say: Out with the old, in with the new!

That's what New Year's is all about—that, and having the biggest party of the year!

The Invite!

Start your New Year's party off right with an invite that finds out what's old and new with your best buds! This invite is a fun questionnaire that your guests will need to return to you by the day before the party so you can all play a hilarious game! (More about this later.) Use the questions below or make up your own.

What's New with Me?

I'm Throwing a Fab Party to Bring in the New Year!

Where: _____

When: _____

But Enough about Me; Tell Me What's New with You!
The best thing that happened to you this year:

_____

_____

The most embarrassing thing that happened to you this year:

_____

Your New Year's resolution is:

_____

Your prediction for yourself for the New Year:

_____

R. S. V. P.

The Setup!

All things glittery and bold are the order for this night! Decorate the party room with big, shimmery balloons and streamers in a mix of silver or gold and deep jewel colors.

Set up a station where your friends can have their fortunes told! Ask an adult to dress the part of a "psychic seer" with hoop earrings, scarves, and flowing skirts, and stock the table with a crystal ball.

Cover one wall with a huge piece of craft paper and set out colorful markers so that guests can xpress their good wishes for the New Year!

Guess Which Guest!

When you've collected all the questionnaires from your friends, make a list of questions based on their answers. For example, if someone wrote that her most embarrassing moment in the past year was when she tripped and fell down the stairs in front of her secret crush, one question could be:

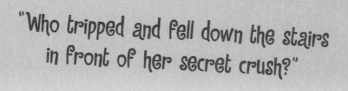

"Who tripped and fell down the stairs in front of her secret crush?"

_____

(name)

Give each guest a copy of the questions and have everyone write down the person that they think each question belongs to.

Read the questions and the correct answers out loud so people can see how well they guessed.

Give a prize to the person with the most right answers. You can even read some of the wrong guesses out loud for fun!

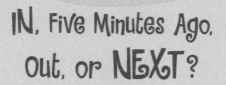

IN, Five Minutes Ago, Out, or NEXT?

Before the party, cut out pictures of different fashion items like clothes, shoes, and accessories; you can even gather pictures of popular celebrities, cartoon characters, or video games. Now you and your best pals can be the fashion police: Hold up each picture and let the group decide what's (or who's) in right now, what's becoming passé, what's definitely **OUT**, and what's on the verge of being the next big thing. What better way to plan your next look? Go with the group or strike out on your own—**it's all up to you!**

Dance Mania!

Start the New Year as a trendsetter in another way—by creating the newest dance sensations! Play the hottest dance tracks of the past year and have a dance contest. Only this contest has a fun twist: Each contestant must try to create the best dance in different categories, for example, Dance Step Most Likely to Get You Mistaken for a Tasmanian Devil or Coolest-Looking Moves I'd Actually Perform in Front of Other People. **Guaranteed to be hilarious!**

The Eats!

Bubbly and festive, sparkling apple cider (or sparkling white grape juice) is the perfect drink to celebrate bringing in the New Year. To make it even more special, serve it in plastic "champagne" glasses over these surprisingly delicious ice cubes. Each one has a treat inside!

Festive Ice Cubes

You will need:

* ice cube trays (regular ones are fine, but it's extra fun if you have trays with molds in cool shapes like hearts or stars!)

* water

* your choice of fresh or canned fruits and berries, such as maraschino cherries, pineapple chunks, orange wedges, and strawberries

* mint leaves

Fill the ice cube trays one-third full with water. Place them in the freezer and then remove when the water is partially frozen. Place a well-drained piece of fruit or a berry and a mint leaf in each cube section. Fill the tray with water and freeze completely.

stand-Up with Style!

LET'S GET THE LAUGHTER STARTED!

Nothing looks as good on a girl as a smile!

That's why this comedy party goes great with my outfit!

12

The Invite!

To put your pals in a laughing mood, send them a joke—
or at least half a joke.

On the front side of your invitation write:

What's the best kind of
panty hose for
baseball players to wear?

Then, on the back of the invitation, write:

For some comic relief (and for the
punchline of my joke) please join me at:

Address:_____

Appearing On:____(date)____

Showtime begins at:___(time)___

R . S . V. P.

Of course, when your guests get to the party, they'll expect to learn
that punchline. So hang a sign on your front door that reads:

The kind of panty hose with runs in them!

The neighbors might think you're a little nuts, but your friends
will get the joke!

The Setup!

Here's how to create a chill-out comedy lounge. The first thing you need to do is set up a stage area. You don't need an actual stage, just a place where the performers can be seen well by everyone in the audience. Comedians don't need a lot of props, usually they just need a chair and a microphone.

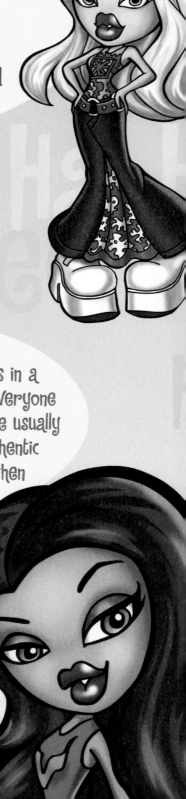

If you don't have a real microphone, just use a round brush. It won't make you sound any louder but it looks really funny—and fashionable!

Now it's time to get the rest of the club ready. Set up chairs in a semi-circle around the stage so everyone can see the action. Comedy clubs are usually dark, so to give your club authentic atmosphere, turn out the lights when the show begins.

Then give each of your guests a flashlight to shine on the stage like a spotlight.

L.O.L. (Lots of Laughs!)

Once all your guests arrive, it's time for the laughs to begin. Take turns going up on stage. You can tell jokes or funny stories, make weird faces, or even perform a whole comedy routine.

Here's one of my favorite stand-up routines. You can use it at your party, or xpress yourself with one of your own!

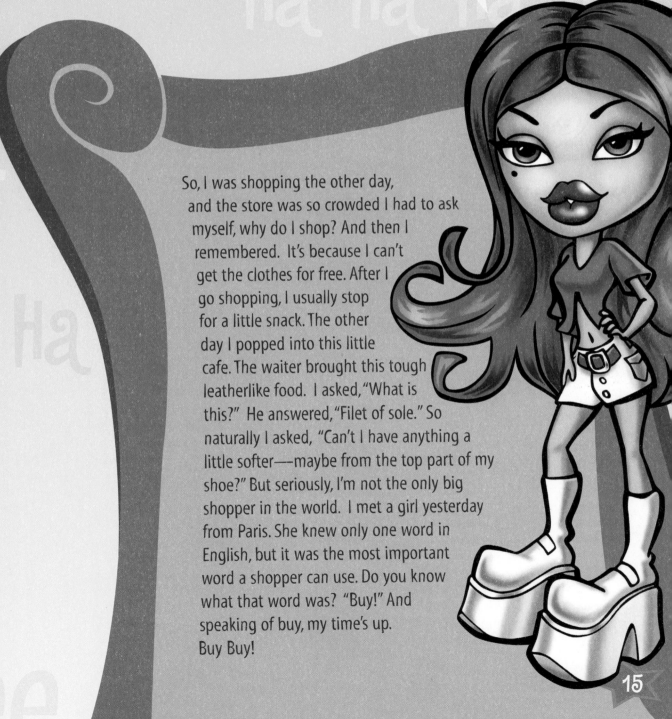

So, I was shopping the other day, and the store was so crowded I had to ask myself, why do I shop? And then I remembered. It's because I can't get the clothes for free. After I go shopping, I usually stop for a little snack. The other day I popped into this little cafe. The waiter brought this tough leatherlike food. I asked, "What is this?" He answered, "Filet of sole." So naturally I asked, "Can't I have anything a little softer—maybe from the top part of my shoe?" But seriously, I'm not the only big shopper in the world. I met a girl yesterday from Paris. She knew only one word in English, but it was the most important word a shopper can use. Do you know what that word was? "Buy!" And speaking of buy, my time's up. Buy Buy!

The Eats!

To give the drinks fashion flair, put a little paper umbrella in each glass.

The Comedy Cocktail

You will need:
- 6-ounces of lemonade concentrate
- 3 cans of water (you can just take the empty cans and fill them up three times)
- 3 ripe pears
- a blender

Have an adult cut the pears in half, remove the cores, and carve them into thin slices. Whirl one cup of sliced pears in the blender until smooth. Add the lemonade concentrate and water. Finally, add the remaining pears. Blend again until the entire mixture is smooth. Pour into glasses and serve. Makes four drinks.

Tongue Ticklin' Pizzas

You will need:

- half of a pita bread for each girl (slice the pita in half and open so that there is a pocket)
- a jar of tomato sauce
- shredded mozzarella cheese
- sliced pepperoni
- chopped red pepper
- sliced mushrooms
- chopped onion
- oregano
- garlic powder

It's every girl for herself when it comes to piling on her favorite pizza toppings. Ask an adult to preheat the oven to 350 degrees. As soon as the custom-made pizzas are complete, have an adult place them in the oven. Bake the pizzas until the cheese melts and the sauce is hot. Remove and serve while hot.

Glam Party!

This fashion fiesta is specially designed for girls with that special inner sense…fashion sense!

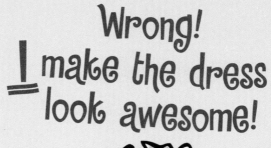

That dress makes you look awesome!

Wrong! <u>I</u> make the dress look awesome!

The Invite!

It won't take much to get the girls in the mood for a night of style, surprise, and fashion design ... your pack is always ready for that! But these super-stylin' invites will be sure to get the fun underway.

Start by gathering up all the fashion mags you can find. Tear off the front covers of enough magazines so that each guest will receive one cover. Now, carefully cut the model's face from each cover. Using a brightly colored marker, write the words "Your Face Here" where the model's face used to be. Then, tape a blank piece of 8"X10" paper to the back of the magazine cover.

Here's what to write on the paper:

Teen Queen Magazine

YOUR FACE HERE

You're invited to a
Glam Party
at _____'s house.
Fashionable Address:

Fiesta Date:

We'll start Glammin' it up at:

Bring your least fave outfit
and least fave accessory!

R. S. V. P.

From Trash to Treasure!

Did that invite say least favorite outfit?

Chill out! One girl's trash is another girl's treasure.

Once your guests have arrived, take all that stuff from the backs of their closets and sort it into piles of tops, bottoms, dresses, shoes, and accessories. Have each girl pull a name from a hat; then she has to dress whomever she picks! The idea is for each "stylist" to transform old duds into stylin' new outfits by putting together a one-of-a-kind ensemble that any fashion diva would be proud to wear! After all, with a little creative mixing and matching, one girl's fashion disaster can become another girl's most stylin' stuff!

When everyone's been given a new look, have a funky fashion show. Take lots of pictures so you can give each girl a photo of her fashion makeover. Your pals will leave with a party keepsake and a cool new outfit. You genius you!

The Eats!

Jade's Passion Fruit Punch

You will need:

- 4 cups cranberry juice
- 3 cups apple juice
- ½ cup fresh lemon juice
- 1 cup pineapple tidbits
- 1 bottle club soda

Mix all the juices together in a big bowl. Add the pineapple tidbits. Pour in the club soda right before serving time. Stir and serve over ice.

Sasha's Sassy Strawberries

You will need:

- 1 pint large ripe strawberries
- 6 ounces chocolate chips
- a saucepan
- wax paper

Wash the berries in cool water and gently pat them dry. Ask an adult to slowly melt the chocolate chips in a pan. When the chips are melted, carefully dip the berries in the chocolate halfway. Place the dipped berries on waxed paper to cool. Arrange the berries on a serving platter and refrigerate until it's time to eat.

21

Today's Homework:
Let the Party Rule!

Celebrate the end of school with a party that proves girls rule!

It's party time!

school's out for summer!

The Invite!

Nothing says "see you in September" more than signing autograph books. To get your friends in the mood for a post-school bash, send them each an autograph book with their invitation.

School's Out. This Party Is In!

Address:

See you on:

Party Time:

R.S.V.P.

P.S. Party homework: This autograph book is a must-have at my party!

Say It with Style!

Looking for something special to write in your buds' books? A statement that'll stand out in the crowd? Well, the girls have gathered some of their favorite autograph rhymes. Because when it comes to friendship, these girls never run out of things to say!

I've **ALWAYS** got something to say.

Don't we **KNOW** it!

Yours 'til Niagara Falls!

IT TICKLES ME, AND MAKES ME LAUGH
TO THINK YOU WANT MY AUTOGRAPH!

Yours 'til the banana splits!

I love you bip,
I love you bop.
I love you more
than hip loves hop!

You asked me to write,
So what shall it be?
Just these two little words,
Remember me.

You are always so cool And ahead of fashion
I'm signing my name With a lot of passion!

CRUISIN' THE SCHOOL HALLS
WAS ALWAYS A TREAT.
KNOWING I'D SEE YOU
MADE IT SO SWEET!

More Signature Party Ideas!

Signature Style

Autograph books are for signing. So why not give the cover of your book a bit of your own signature style? Start your party with this artsy project! **You will need:** Fashion magazines, sports magazines (so that the boys at the party can personalize their autograph books as well!), and any awesome catalogues you have lying around your house. You can stylize your autograph book with cool cut-out pictures! Give your friends a chance to xpress themselves by decorating their autograph books. Just be sure you wait 'til the glue and paint are dry before you trade books and **start your signing**.

Homework: Extra Credit!

Decorate your party room with memories of the school year that's past. Make posters using photos from school plays, presentations, and field trips.

Tape your posters to the walls. Your friends will have a blast looking back on all the fun you guys had this year.

For a little extra credit, tie helium balloons to all the chairs at your party table. Use a red marker to write these words on the balloons: **Grade A+**

The Eats!

Since you don't have to save your apples for the teacher anymore, whip up this apple treat for you and your buds!

A+ Apple Smoothee!

You will need:

- 1 pint vanilla ice cream
- 1 quart naturally sweet apple cider
- freshly ground nutmeg
- blender
- an adult to help

Let the pint of vanilla ice cream soften at room temperature or microwave for 20 seconds. Put the softened ice cream and cider in a blender and ask an adult to blend until frothy and well mixed. Stir in nutmeg and serve in tall glasses. Makes 6 one-cup servings.

Come One, Come All, Carnival!

GAMES! FACE PAINTING! FOOD!

It's easy to turn your backyard into a fun and funky carnival.

Just follow these directions to xpress your inner party girl!

The Invite!

To get your guests in the carnival mood before they even arrive, design your invitation to look like the tickets they give out at carnivals. Then tape your invite to a bag of peanuts, popcorn, or cotton candy (just to give your guests a little taste of the fun to come!).

ADMIT ONE
You're Invited!
_____

Carnival Party at
_____'s house.

Address: _____

The Games Begin on:_____ (date)

Meet at:_____ (time)

R. S. V. P.

Got Game?

What's a carnival without games? Here are a few traditional carnival games—with a passionate twist—that you can set up in your backyard.

For added atmosphere, ask an adult to act as a balloon man, giving out helium balloons to your guests as they travel through the carnival!

FACE PAINTING!

No carnival would be complete without a funky face painting booth. Ask an adult or older sib to play Picasso, and give your guests a whole new look. Here are some ways to Xpress yourself with face paint:

- rainbows
- peace sign
- hearts
- smiley faces
- stars

- the sun
- shoes
- moon
- jewels

Sweet scented lip glosses would make a great prize at this booth.

Lip Gloss Toss

All you need for this booth is:

- 6 fish bowls
- water
- 3 lip glosses (all the same size)
- a table

Set the bowls on the table so they look like this:

Fill the bowls with water. Have your guests stand at least six feet from the table. One by one ask them to toss the lip gloss containers at the bowls. If a contestant gets three lip gloss containers into the fish bowls, she wins!

Super Soaker

Caution! You will get wet!

For this wet and wacky game you'll need:

- 6 sponges
- 1 bucket of water
- an empty bucket
- a garden chair

Start by soaking the sponges in the bucket of water. As the hostess, you get to sit in the lounge chair. You should sit with your back to your guests so you can't see what's coming. Then hold the empty bucket on top of your head. Once you're settled in, ask your guests to line up at least six feet from you. It's their job to throw the wet sponges in your direction. If a guest gets the sponge in the bucket, she wins!

FASHION FLURRY

Gather up shirts, jeans, skirts, socks, shoes, scarves, handbags, and hats. Place them in a huge pile. Divide all your guests into two teams. Each team will choose one player to be the model. The other players will be the dressers.

Ask an adult to be the official judge. As soon as the judge says go, the dressers on both teams should begin picking through the pile of clothes, trying to come up with a fashionable outfit for their model to wear. Each outfit should include one of each of the following:

▸ **top**

▸ **bottom (pants or a skirt)**   ▸ **scarf**

▸ **matching socks (or not)**   ▸ **shoes**

▸ **pocketbook**

▸ **hat**

The first team to get their model completely dressed wins the game.

Give each girl on the winning team a beaded friendship bracelet or a funky hair accessory as a prize!

the Eats!

Everyone loves carnival food. Make sure you have plenty of hot dogs, ice cream, and soda on hand so that people can munch all day long. And of course, no carnival's complete without **popcorn**! To give your corn some extra pop, give your guests a choice of popper toppers.

Here's all you do: Before the party begins, prepare a table of popper toppers. Fill small bowls with things that taste yummy over popcorn. Once you've prepared the toppers, give each girl a bag of popcorn. Let her spoon on the toppers she likes the best. Then shake the bag and eat!

Peanuts and popcorn are an earthy snack I can sink my teeth into.

A little chili powder adds just the kick I need.

I like cinnamon and sugar. It's sweet like me!

Popcorn with grated parmesan cheese is totally far out!

Freaky, Funky Halloween!

Are you ready to throw the most gruesomely groovy Halloween party ever?
Let the girls show you how!

The Invite!

To let your guests know that they're about to have a haunting good time, start by creating an invitation that will creep them out . . . not **keep** them out! Begin by cutting a piece of paper into the shape of a bat. Then use a blood-red pen to write out your information.

Come for a Scare . . . if You Dare!

It's a Halloween Party at _____'s house.
Where to go if you dare to show:
Don't be late on this date:
Time to beware!:
R . S . V . P .

That's all the important info. But your invite's not quite right. . .

To finish it off, roll the invitation into a thin tube.
Slip the tube into either a black or orange balloon.
Blow up the balloons, seal them up, and give one
to each of your friends with a note that says:

"Pop me—if you dare!"

Have You Got a Passion for Fashion?

Wanna look like the Pack this Halloween? Here's how:

Be a Kool Kat like me in a cat suit in the color of your choice. Just add a long cat tail and sport a headband with cat ears . . . and purrrr!

They don't call me Pretty Princess for nothing! And since that's what I am, a sparkly tiara and a pretty-in-pink ball gown is the perfect ensemble for me this Halloween!

To get my angelic appeal, a sparkly white dress, feathered wings, and a halo (what else?) are all you need. Some may think the spice of Halloween is in the tricks, but we know that sweetness is the real treat, and twice as nice!

If you want to be like Bunny Boo, wear a body suit with soft furry accents at the neck, cuffs, and pants hem, then make a headband with long bunny ears. So what are you waiting for? Hop to it!

Happy Haunting!

BEWARE! THIS IS THE HOUSE OF HAUNT!

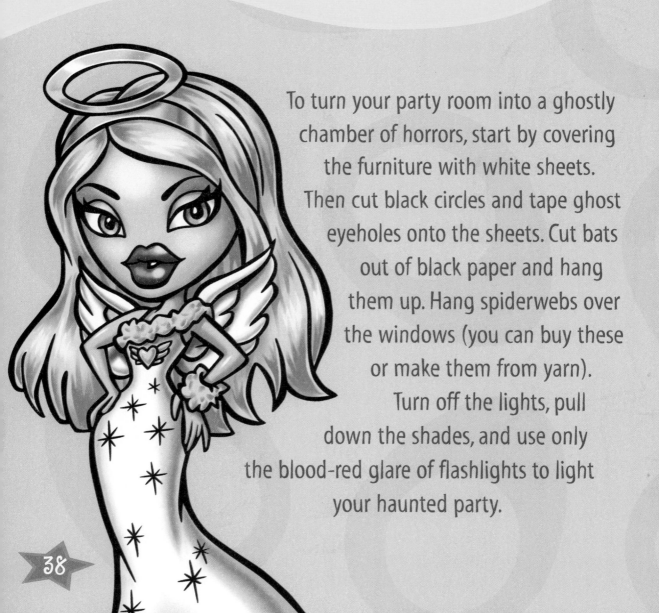

To turn your party room into a ghostly chamber of horrors, start by covering the furniture with white sheets. Then cut black circles and tape ghost eyeholes onto the sheets. Cut bats out of black paper and hang them up. Hang spiderwebs over the windows (you can buy these or make them from yarn). Turn off the lights, pull down the shades, and use only the blood-red glare of flashlights to light your haunted party.

The Tour of TERROR!

It's time to prepare your Finger Frights. These containers of disgusting things are specially designed to gross out the guests!

Bowl of Eyeballs: Peel 30 grapes and put them in a bowl.

Bag of Guts: Fill a plastic bag with cooked spaghetti or macaroni that has been allowed to cool.

Platter of Fingers: Place piles of cooked carrots or small pickles on a plate.

Bat Brains: A bowl of cold mashed potatoes with lots of lumps.

Witches' Hearts: A bowl of chilled stewed prunes.

Dead Man's Bones: A stack of dried sticks left on the floor.

As soon as all of your Finger Frights are prepared, turn off the lights in your party room, and turn on a recording of the creepiest music you can find. Now wait for your ghouls . . . er . . . guests to arrive. Once all of your victims are at the party, give them a "hands-on" tour of the Finger Frights. Give each guest a blindfold and ask them to feel each gross goodie that you've prepared. Make sure you tell them that they're feeling eyeballs, guts, fingers, hearts, brains, and bones. Use your scariest voice, to really creep them out. And make sure they wash their hands afterward! You don't want all your guests walking around with sticky fingers!

Handle with fear!

39

THE EATS!

When it comes to Halloween food, the grosser the better! Here are some ghoulishly good recipes that taste a whole lot better than they look!

Look at what we've cooked up!

These are ooey, gooey, and good, but you'll need an adult to help you heat them up.

Gummy Pond Scum

You will need:
* 1 package green jelly (four serving size)
* 4 clear plastic cups
* 1 bag jelly snakes

Prepare the jelly according to the directions on the package. Pour the jelly into the clear cups in four equal sized servings. Once the jelly is almost set, add jelly snakes to the top and serve. Makes four servings of pond scum.

Chocolate Worms

You will need:

- 1 small bag of chocolate chips
- 1 small bag of butterscotch chips
- wax paper
- bowl
- 1 can of crunchy Chinese noodles
- wooden spoon
- bowl
- saucepan

Get an adult to melt the chocolate and butterscotch chips together in a saucepan. Pour the melted chips into the bowl. Dump the noodles into the bowl and stir carefully. Drop spoonfuls of the mixture of candy-coated noodles onto the wax paper. Allow your worms to cool before serving.

I just love chocolate worms—with a side of eyeballs, of course!

Bloody Eyeballs

You will need:

- 6 peeled hard boiled eggs
- 6 ounces whipped cream cheese
- 12 green olives stuffed with pimentos
- ketchup
- toothpicks

Ask an adult to cut the eggs in half widthwise. Remove the yolks and fill the holes with cream cheese. Smooth out the surface of the cream cheese as much as possible. Press one olive, pimento side up, into the cream cheese of each eyeball. This will give you a ghoulish green iris with a blood red pupil. Dip a toothpick into the ketchup and use it to draw broken blood vessels into the cream cheese. Makes 12 eyeballs.

Funk 'N' Glow™ on the Go!

Everyone gets a new look at this movin' on makeover party that's guaranteed to put the fun in funky! Funk 'N' Glow™ on the Go is a progressive party. That means that the party moves from house to house throughout the evening. Each girl gets to host part of the party at her house.

At our movin' on makeover parties, we always start at my house to soothe our skin with creams.

My room is the hairdo headquarters.

Then it's on to my house for manicures and pedicures.

And of course, we finish up at my house, cuz I've got the biggest selection of make-up.

To put your pals in the makeover mood, send your invitation wrapped around a mini hairbrush. That's sure to get their attention. Here's what to write on the invite:

Let's Have a Movin' On Makeover!

Date:_____

Time to get beautified: _____

Your house will be

our ___1ST_____2ND_____3RD_____4TH_____stop.

(circle one)

You will be in charge of

(check one)

☐ facials
☐ manicures
☐ hair
☐ make-up

Don't forget the munchies!

43

Houses of Beauty!

Give each girl a disposable camera, so you can take before and after pics!

House 1:
Skin Care

You will need:
- alcohol-free skin cleansers
- cotton balls
- aromatherapy face creams
- thin cucumber slices

Get the party started by taking "before pictures" of each other. Then clean your face by applying the cleanser with cotton balls and rinsing thoroughly. Next, rub a thin layer of face cream into your skin. Finally, lie flat on your back and place one cucumber slice over each eye and rest for five minutes, giving the cool cucumbers a chance to reduce any swelling under your eyes. Then wash your face with warm water, and move on to the next house.

44

House 2:
Manicures

You will need:

- nail polish remover
- cotton balls
- cotton swabs
- emery boards
- clear polish
- several light shades of polish
- nail stickers

You might be here a while! Try renting a funky fashion movie to make the time fly by!

Pair off into groups of two to give each other manicures. Before you begin, allow everyone to choose their favorite polish and stickers. Be sure to clean off all the old nail polish before starting a new manicure. Don't move on to the next house until everyone's nails are completely dry.

Scissors are off limits! Leave the cutting to the experts.

House 3:
Hair Stylin'

- towels
- hair gels
- hairspray
- rinse-out color
- clips
- hair-bands
- hair glitter
- one blow dryer for every two girls

Each guest should bring her own hairbrush.

Take turns wetting your hair in the sink. It's easier to work with wet hair than dry. Then use the gel, brushes, and blow dryers to create new styles for each other. Finish off the look with clips, color spray, and glitter.

Here's a word to the wise: Don't share lipsticks or eyeliners. Some things are meant to be kept private—keep your germs to yourself!

House 4:
Make-up Madness

You will need:
* A variety of lip glosses in different colors and flavors
* blush
* a variety of eye shadows
* body glitter
* make-up sponges

To keep the makeover excitement brewing, keep the party room free of mirrors until everyone has had a chance to be made up by someone else. Then, when everyone is makeover magnificent, bring out the mirrors for the big reveal!

Don't forget to pull out your camera and snap lots of "after pictures" so you and your pals will always remember how hot you looked!

The Eats!

Each host should prepare simple snacks and drinks ahead of time. For example, serve fresh veggies at **House 1**; fruit smoothees at **House 2**—served with straws, of course, to keep wet nails safe!; and popcorn and pretzels at **House 3**. And for **House 4**, here's a sweet treat to eat at the end of your travels along the beauty highway!

This fruit fondue is fun to do!

At our parties, even the fruit gets a makeover!

Funky Fondue

You will need:
- 1 cup plain yogurt
- 2 tablespoons thawed frozen orange juice concentrate
- small bowl of brown sugar
- raspberries
- fresh strawberries
- banana slices
- grapes
- apple chunks
- pear chunks
- pineapple chunks
- toothpicks
- bowl

Mix the yogurt and the juice concentrate together in a bowl. Put the fruit on a platter and place a toothpick in each piece. Have your guests dip each piece of fruit in the fondue mixture and then roll it in the sugar. Yum!

This book is over, but you can keep partying!
Using the ideas in the guide for inspiration,
come up with your own funky—
and fashionable—party themes!

Be creative,
be unique, be you—
and PARTY ON!